LOST IN THE TUNNEL OF TIME

Welcome to This Book

It's not easy to be brave when you're scared. It's even harder when you're in danger. Ziggy and his friends know this all too well.

Ziggy, Rico, Rashawn, and Jerome are trapped in an old dirt tunnel. The secret tunnel was part of the Underground Railroad. It was used by African Americans escaping slavery nearly 150 years ago. Ziggy learned about the tunnel after finding an old map. Then he and his friends, known as The Black Dinosaurs, decided to explore it.

Will they survive their adventure into the past?

Target Words

These words will help you understand how Ziggy and his friends get *Lost in the Tunnel of Time*.

- **daring:** risky
  Ziggy and his friends are always up for a daring adventure.
- **mysterious:** very hard to explain or understand
  They follow a mysterious map that leads to a tunnel beneath their school.
- **route:** a path or course
  The tunnel is part of an old route on the Underground Railroad.

Reader Tips

Here's how to get the most out of this book.

- **Illustrations** Look at the illustration of Ziggy and his friends on page 32. Keep the picture in mind as you read about the boys' adventure to help you keep track of the characters.
- **Setting** Notice details in the story that tell when and where the story takes place. The setting can make characters act in certain ways or cause events or problems to happen.

This book is dedicated to
Liza Glasper
Annette Randle
Whitney Randle
Stephan Hudson
Kwami Agyeman
Kwabema Agyeman

Special thanks to
E. Selean Hudson
Director of African-American Programs Museum Center
Cincinnati Historical Society
and
The Bernstein Family of B.B. Riverboats

Printed in the U.S.A.

ISBN 0-439-58868-5

7 8 9 10 23 12 11 10 09

and

The Black Dinosaurs™

LOST IN THE TUNNEL OF TIME

by Sharon M. Draper

illustrated by Michael Bryant

SCHOLASTIC INC.

New York Toronto London Auckland Sydney

Mexico City New Delhi Hong Kong Buenos Aires

About the Author

If you were to ask Sharon M. Draper how often she writes, her answer would probably be, "whenever I get the chance." Ms. Draper's love for writing and literature is clearly evident from the stories she writes for her own children to the vast knowledge of literature she—as chair of the Walnut Hills High School English Department and English Literature teacher—passes on to her students.

A graduate of Pepperdine University, Ms. Draper's literary recognition began when she won first prize in the Gertrude H. Johnson Williams Literary Contest and had her short story, "One Small Torch," published in *Ebony* magazine. She was also recipient of the first Genesis Award for her YA novel, *Tears of A Tiger.* It was presented by the Coretta Scott King Award Committee of the American Library Association to recognize work of literary merit by a new writer.

Ms. Draper lives in Cincinnati, Ohio with her husband and four children and is working on several additional adventure stories for the *Ziggy and The Black Dinosaurs* series.

About the Illustrator

Michael Bryant is a native of Newark, New Jersey. He attended Clifford Scott High School in East Orange and received his bachelor's degree from Kean College in New Jersey. Mr. Bryant was the winner of the University of Wisconsin Multicultural Mirror Fellowship in 1991 and is a mentor at the Center for Multicultural Children's Literature in New York City.

Michael Bryant has illustrated a number of books for children including *Treemonisha* and *Our People*, both writtten by Angela Shelf Medearis. *Ziggy and The Black Dinosaurs: Lost in the Tunnel of Time* is the first title he has illustrated for Just Us Books. Mr. Bryant lives in Newark, New Jersey with his wife and their two daughters.

Contents

Chapter 1

Like cool, sweet milk on a bowl of crunchy cereal, the Thursday morning breeze splashed the crisp, dry leaves under Rico's feet. He liked this time of year. It would soon be time for warm fires in the fireplace and frosty snow on the sidewalk. His mom had made him wear a jacket to school today and it felt good. As he walked across the street to the school building, he spotted his friend Ziggy and waved.

Ziggy sat on the front steps of the school, digging wildly in his book bag. He pulled out two broken pencils; a half-eaten apple; a red spiral notebook; a sandwich wrapped in plastic; a doorknob; and a green tennis shoe. "Hey, Rico-mon! Did you do your history homework?"

Rico chuckled. "Sure, Ziggy. It was easy. Didn't you do yours?"

"Of course I did it, mon—Ziggy is no fool. But I can't *find* it!"

Ziggy continued to empty the contents of his book bag on the school steps—his math book, seven small smooth rocks, five nickels, and a purple three-ring binder. "It's gotta be in here somewhere," he mumbled to himself. His long braided hair hung over his shoulders, covered with a small red and green knitted cap.

"What are the rocks for?" asked Rico.

"I just call them the 'Seven Special Stones,'" replied Ziggy mysteriously as he held the rocks in his hand for Rico to see.

"How do you know they're so special?"

"Sh-sh!" Ziggy whispered. "Can you keep a secret, mon?"

"Sure," replied Rico, who never knew what Ziggy would do or say.

"These stones . . .," Ziggy paused for a moment. He looked around to make sure no one was listening. His voiced dropped to a whisper. "These stones keep away *ghosts*!"

"Ghosts?" Rico laughed nervously. "There are no ghosts around here!"

"See how well the stones are working, mon?"

Ziggy replied with glee. Rico laughed again, shaking his head at his friend. Ziggy plopped the stones back into his book bag.

Just then a gust of wind blew through the schoolyard and across the steps. The pages of Ziggy's red notebook fluttered, and gently released the one sheet of paper that had been tucked inside. Ziggy's large, round handwriting boldly filled both sides of the paper.

Ziggy grabbed it triumphantly. "I found it, mon! Let the bells ring and the school day begin!"

The early bell seemed to hear him, for the signal to go into the building sounded just as he spoke. Ziggy stuffed the rest of his things back into his bag, tossed it over his shoulder, and called to Rico, who never ceased to be amazed at Ziggy, "Let's go, mon—we'll be late!"

Their school building was very old. It had five floors of classrooms with a large marble staircase leading from the front door on the main floor to the upper floors. The long, dark hallways were shiny with wax and worn footsteps.

As Rico and Ziggy reached their lockers on the third floor, they saw Rashawn and Jerome sitting on the floor waiting for them.

"What's up?" yawned Rashawn. He uncurled his long legs, stood up, and stretched. He had grown taller during the long summer vacation, and was proud that his size ten shoes were the biggest. Lots of people said he looked like Michael Jordan. He liked that.

"Nothin' much," replied Rico. "Ziggy was having a homework attack, but he found it."

"So what else is new?" chuckled Jerome. "Ziggy loses his homework every day."

"It's not always my fault," replied Ziggy with a cheerful sigh. "Monday it was the jelly's fault, Tuesday it was my mum's fault, and Wednesday it was the cat's fault!"

"How do you figure?" asked Rico.

"It's simple, mon. Somehow, when I made my bologna and jelly sandwich, the jelly jumped up, landed on my math homework, and made my paper stick to the bottom of my book bag! The next day, my mum washed my favorite blue jeans with my science homework in the back pocket."

"I know you're gonna tell us," laughed Jerome, "but how did the cat lose your homework?"

"She didn't lose it, mon—she attacked it!"

"What?"

"My cat's name is Jungle Kitty. She runs around the house, acting like she's a lion or tiger, and attacking dangerous creatures like shoes and pieces of paper."

"What if she saw a mouse?" asked Rashawn.

"She'd probably run the other way, mon," Ziggy laughed. "But she really had fun beating up my homework paper that night!"

"Did Jungle Kitty get last night's history homework, too?" Jerome asked.

"No way, mon. This one was too important. It tried to hide from me, but I knew where it was all the time. There's no way I'm gonna miss that field trip!"

Mrs. Powell, their history teacher, was taking them on an all-day field trip to the Ohio River. Only the students who turned in their homework would be allowed to go, so Ziggy and the rest of the class had been extra careful to have it ready.

Jerome was shorter than Rashawn, but was strong and tough looking. His face was brown and leathery, like the brown leather bomber jacket that he wore every day. He checked his book bag for his homework, and grinned at the other boys. "This is gonna be an awesome field trip—lunch on the river bank, and a boat ride!"

"You got that right," replied Rico with excitement. He was neatly dressed in dark blue shorts and a light blue shirt. His coffee-colored, smiling face was surrounded by thick, curly brown hair. His book bag, unlike the other boys', was neat and organized. His history homework was always in his green history folder, and his math homework was always in his blue math folder. He liked to draw pictures of houses and kept those drawings in a special red folder—he said that one day he'd like to be an architect.

Mrs. Powell came around the corner jiggling keys and balancing a coffee cup on a large stack of papers just as the bell rang to begin class.

"Looks like I made it just in time," she cried cheerfully. "I was making last minute plans for our trip," she explained as she unlocked the classroom door. "Now where did he go? He was right behind me."

"Who?" asked Jerome.

"Oh, there he is! Come on in, Mr. Greene. Welcome to our classroom."

Mr. Greene walked slowly around the corner. He was almost bald, with wisps of curly, gray hair and golden-copper, slightly wrinkled skin. His dark eyes twinkled as he saw Rico, Rashawn, Jerome, and Ziggy standing in the hallway, staring in surprise.

"Well, if it isn't The Black Dinosaurs!" chuckled Mr. Greene. "Good to see you again!"

Chapter 2

"Hey, Mr. Greene! What are you doing here, mon?" asked Ziggy.

"Your teacher asked me to go along on your field trip today," replied Mr. Greene with a smile.

"Why would an old dude like you want to go on a trip with a bunch of kids?" Rico asked.

"Just wait and see," whispered Mr. Greene with mystery in his voice. "But tell me about you—have you had any meetings of The Black Dinosaurs lately?"

"The Black Dinosaurs" was the name of the club that Ziggy, Rashawn, Rico, and Jerome had started last summer. They had built a clubhouse in Ziggy's back yard, and Mr. Greene had once helped them solve a mystery about a buried box of bones.

"Sure, mon," replied Ziggy, "but since school has

started, we usually only meet on Saturday. Stop by some time and see us. I'm bringing peanut-butter pizza this week!"

Mr. Greene grabbed his throat, pretended to gag, and groaned, "No thanks—not this time."

Rico and Jerome giggled, and Rashawn whispered, "If Ziggy brings it, I'm gonna make him eat the whole thing!"

They walked into the classroom then, talking and laughing, found their seats, and waited to find out why Mr. Greene was at their school.

Mrs. Powell, who was dressed in jeans, a sweatshirt, and tennis shoes, instead of her usual suit and black, patent-leather heels, was in a good mood. She took attendance, collected the homework, and cheered out loud when every single homework paper was turned in.

"Class, the bus is here. Be sure you have your lunch with you. Let's go! Mr. Greene, it's right this way, sir."

They all trooped noisily down the stairs, while Mrs. Powell whispered loudly, "Hush! You'll disturb the other classes." Nobody really got any quieter, but at least she tried. Mrs. Powell checked names as each person got on the bus, and when everyone was seated, the bus roared away from the school while the children inside cheered.

Ziggy was sitting next to Rico and right behind Mr. Greene and Mrs. Powell. "So what's going on, mon?" he whispered in Mr. Greene's ear.

"I like the river," replied Mr. Greene.

"You like it so much that you got on a school bus full of kids just to see it?" asked Rico. "You could have walked down to the river from your house."

"I often do, Rico," replied Mr. Greene. "Sometimes before daybreak I walk down here and watch the morning wake up and the day begin its business. It's a wonderful sight."

"Awesome, mon," replied Ziggy as he settled back into his seat.

The bus ride was short, for the school was not very far from the river. The first stop was Eden Park. The weather was just a little chilly, but the bright sunlight made the day seem warm and cheerful. The trees had lost most of their leaves; they looked as if they might shiver when the warmth of the sun left for the night.

The children trooped off the bus, walked through the park a short ways, then stopped at a low stone wall. Suddenly there was silence. Fifty feet below them, shining in the sunlight, was the Ohio River.

"Wow!" whispered Rashawn. "My mom and dad and I have driven over the bridge lots of times, but all you can really see from the car window is a little bit of dirty brown water. I never knew the river was pretty!"

Silent and powerful, and filled with dark mysteries, the river relaxed at their feet. Like a long, purple serpent, it curled lazily as it wound its way from there to wherever. Although it was crossed by bridges and dotted with boats and barges, the river seemed strong, as if it were ignoring the dirt and pollution of the present, and remembering the glory of its past.

"That's Kentucky, isn't it, Mrs. Powell?" asked Rico, pointing to the buildings across the river. "It seems like it's close enough to touch, but it also seems like it's a million miles away."

"You're right, Rico, and I know what you mean," Mrs. Powell agreed. "When we get on the boat this afternoon, you will be able to see how far away and yet how close it really is."

Suddenly Ziggy exclaimed, "There's our boat! Look! It says *BB Riverboats*! They're loading up! We're gonna miss it, mon!"

"Calm down, Ziggy," replied Mrs. Powell with patience. "We don't have to be on our boat for another hour. They won't leave without us. I promise."

As the children sat and stood near the wall, the river seemed to make them quiet as they listened to its silent story.

"This is nice," said Jerome quietly. "The wind is blowing, the sun is shining, and there's no bugs!"

"I bet if that old river could talk, he'd have some mighty stories to tell," Rico said thoughtfully.

"Is the water very deep?" asked Nicole, a girl with long black braids and a questioning look constantly on her face. Rico thought she looked confused. Jerome thought she looked cute. Ziggy hadn't noticed her at all.

"It sure is," replied Mr. Greene, "very deep and cold. And you're right, Rico. There are some really powerful stories from the river. That's why I'm here today."

"True stories?" asked Tiana, a tall, thin, toffee-tanned girl. She moved closer to Rashawn, who was the only boy in class taller than she was. Rashawn pretended he didn't notice and looked only at Mr. Greene.

"Oh, yes—very true," replied Mr. Greene. "My daddy and my granddaddy both grew up down here on the river. My granddaddy worked on the big riverboats that went from here all the way down to the Mississippi River to New Orleans. And my daddy worked on the docks, lifting and loading all of his life. From the time I was a very small boy, they told me stories from the river—tales of sailors and chases and losers and lovers."

At the word "lovers," Tiana edged one step closer to Rashawn. He pretended he had to sneeze and moved one step away.

"Tell us about some of the chases, mon!" cried Ziggy with excitement.

Rashawn quickly joined in. "Yeah! We want to hear some adventure stories!" The rest of the class loudly agreed. Tiana sighed. She whispered to Nicole that she'd rather hear some of the love stories. Nicole smiled and nodded her head.

"Did you know," asked Mr. Greene, "that the Ohio River was a major route of the Underground Railroad?"

"That's wacko, mon! I thought you said these were true stories!" argued Ziggy.

"What kind of train ran on the river?"

"He said *underground,*" answered Jerome. "But that doesn't make sense either. What kind of railroad goes under the ground or under a river? They didn't have subways back then, did they?"

"Didn't you do your homework?" sniffed Tiffany with a knowing look. "It was all about . . ."

" . . . slaves and stuff!" replied Ziggy. "I know because I finished it while I was watching TV."

"If you had turned off the TV and read the last page, you would have come to the part about the Underground Railroad. Isn't that right, Mrs. Powell?" asked Tiffany, even though she was sure of the answer.

"She's right, Ziggy," smiled Mrs. Powell. "The last part of your homework was to read those pages in the book on the Underground Railroad."

"Oh, no!" cried Ziggy, who smacked himself in the forehead as if he were really upset. "Did you say READ those pages? I thought you said REACH that part! So I reached it, and closed my book. Then I fixed myself a tomato and banana milkshake and went to bed, mon!"

Nobody believed Ziggy, but everyone laughed—even Mrs. Powell. Ziggy grinned, and Mr. Greene

spoke quietly. "I'm going to tell you a tale that you can't find in your history books—because it's a true story. Listen!" he whispered softly. The class gathered in a circle, sat on the grass, and waited for Mr. Greene to begin.

Chapter 3

"The Underground Railroad," Mr. Greene began, "was not a railroad at all. It was a method used to help slaves to escape from the South to the North where they could be free. It was very dangerous, but it was daring and mysterious, too."

"So why was it called a railroad?" asked Rashawn.

"Let me explain. It was run like an invisible train. The escaped slaves had to travel long distances, and they made stops at homes of people who helped them to the next safe place. Folks who didn't understand about the secret hiding places would say that it seemed like the people just *disappeared underground*."

"Awesome, mon!" whispered Ziggy.

"Everything had to be kept secret because it was

against the law for a slave to try to escape and it was also against the law for anyone to help a slave to escape," continued Mr. Greene.

"You mean you'd go to jail for wanting to be free?" asked Nicole with amazement.

"No, you wouldn't go to jail—if you were an escaped slave who was captured, you would go back to your owner and back to slavery—where you would probably be punished severely."

"They'd never catch me!" said Jerome with his head held high.

"Maybe not, Jerome, but many people were."

"How did they travel, Mr. Greene?" asked Nicole.

"Sometimes by wagon, but mostly they traveled on foot."

"You mean they *walked* from way down South to way up North?" asked Jerome with amazement. "I rode in a car with my grandmother and my two loud little sisters from Georgia to Ohio, and it seemed to take forever!"

"Do you know anybody who walked here, Mr. Greene?" asked Mimi, a small, quiet girl sitting on the grass near Rico.

"I sure do, little one," replied Mr. Greene. "That's

why your teacher asked me to come today. My granddaddy, Mac, came to Cincinnati on the Underground Railroad!"

"Well, don't just sit there, mon! Tell us the story!" Ziggy was almost dancing with excitement.

"When Mac was just a little older than you kids are, his mama decided to leave slavery in Georgia and try to get to freedom here in Cincinnati. She had heard her owner say that he was going to sell her, so she left that night with a small pack in one arm, her only son Mac in the other, and a dream in her heart to be free."

"You could sell *people*?" asked Tiana with amazement.

"Yes," Mr. Greene said quietly. "You could sell people. So she left. She walked slowly through the woods each night, following the North Star when the nights were clear, and looking for other signs, like moss on the trees and the direction of flowing streams, when clouds covered the night sky. She was afraid of the sounds and the darkness of the night, but she was more afraid of being captured and returned to slavery. They hid during the day and tried to sleep in the woods with leaves and branches over them. It was very hot and insect bites covered them."

"Bugs?" yelled Jerome. "It must have been awful!"

Mr. Greene chuckled. "The bugs were nothing compared to the hunger. All they had to eat was berries from the woods. Just when they thought they could go no further, a wagon appeared on the road. Mac thought they were captured, but the driver of the wagon was smiling. He took them to his house where he fed them and hid them in a tunnel under his basement for three days."

"Underground! Now I get it!" said Rico.

"That smiling farmer took Mac and his mama to another smiling farmer, who hid them in his barn for a week. I think they must have hidden at seven different homes. Each stop got them closer to the river. When they finally got to the Ohio River. . . "

". . . they got in a car and came across the bridge, mon!" laughed Ziggy.

"Sure Ziggy," smiled Mr. Greene. "None of these bridges had even been built yet. What really happened was they were put in a packing box, addressed to a lady in Cincinnati, and put on a ferry boat to cross the river. The lady was on the other side when they arrived, they were unpacked in Ohio, and were free!"

"Hooray!" the class cheered. "No more problems for Mac and his mama!"

"Not quite," sighed Mr. Greene. "They weren't safe yet. They still had to hide for several weeks until they could get proper papers. If a slave catcher saw them, they could be forced to return to slavery."

"That's not fair!"

"You're right," said Mr. Greene.

"So where did they hide?" Rico wanted to know.

"Well, there were several possibilities," answered Mr. Greene. "There were basements, and attics, and barns that were used as hiding places. Also, many of the houses built back then had secret rooms."

"Secret rooms?" asked Nicole.

"Here in Cincinnati?" Tiana wondered.

"How could a room be secret?" Jerome wanted to know.

"Some rooms were hidden behind walls or under trap doors," replied Mr. Greene. "They were very small. And some were just dirt tunnels that served as a means of escape from the house to the outside."

"So where did Mac and his mama hide?" demanded Rico. "You still didn't tell us."

"They hid," Mr. Greene said quietly and dramatically, "in secret rooms that are located *right underneath your school*!" For a moment, the children were silent with disbelief.

"What do you mean secret rooms under our school?" Jerome finally asked.

"Have you seen any of the secret rooms, Mr. Greene?" Rashawn wanted to know.

"No, Rashawn, I haven't. But my daddy and my granddaddy Mac used to tell me stories about them. You see, an old farm that was a hiding place for the Underground Railroad used to stand where your school is now located. When your school was built almost a hundred years ago, the old tunnels and secret rooms were lost, but not forgotten."

"Is that true, Mrs. Powell?" asked Rico.

"Mr. Greene is the expert on this," replied Mrs. Powell. "I've always heard stories about the secret passageways hidden under our school, but I never really believed them . . . just like the story of the River City Ghost."

"GHOST?! What ghost? Who is the River City Ghost?" All of the children were asking with excitement and a little fear. Rico glanced at Ziggy and shivered.

"The River City Ghost was a story that my grandmother used to tell me when I was just little girl," replied Mrs. Powell. "I'm sure it's just something she made up to make us behave. But the tunnels and the Underground Railroad—those are not make-believe—those are real."

"So there really are tunnels under our school," Jerome remarked. "Amazing!"

"Yes, but those have been covered and lost for over a hundred years," reminded Mr. Greene.

"What about the ghost?" asked Rico. "Will you tell us the story that your grandmother told you, Mrs. Powell?"

"Maybe the River City Ghost lives in one of those lost tunnels, mon!" whispered Ziggy with mystery in his voice.

"It's strange that you should say that, Ziggy," replied Mrs. Powell. "There *is* a tunnel in the story. Maybe there's a connection!"

"Tell us the story, Mrs. Powell," Tiana pleaded. She shivered and moved closer to Rashawn.

"All right," agreed Mrs. Powell. "Listen, children!"

"Awesome, mon," said Ziggy quietly. "Marvelous mysteries all around us!"

Chapter 4

"Late at night, after everyone had gone to bed," Mrs. Powell began, "a strange whistling wind could be heard, blowing from the river, and over the streets of Cincinnati. Sometimes it sounded like a voice; sometimes it sounded like a song."

"Did you ever hear it?" asked Nicole.

"One night, while I was sleeping in my grandma's big, soft feather bed, I heard it, or at least I thought I did."

"Were you scared?"

"No, because I was warm and safe in my grandma's bed. Then she heard that whispering wind also, so she told me the story."

With the wind from the river blowing gently about

them, the children sat spellbound, listening to Mrs. Powell's tale. Mr. Greene, with a twinkle in his eye, smiled at the scene.

Mrs. Powell continued. "Long before there were bridges and highways, about the time that Mr. Greene's grandpa Mac and his mother came here, there lived an old Shawnee Indian woman down by the river. She was about a hundred years old and was very wise. All the river men knew her and looked out for her. They would bring her fish, or cloth, or pretty shells that they collected in their travels on the river. In turn she helped them if they got sick or if they needed a place to sleep.

"Many people said that she also helped escaped slaves, but no one knew for sure. Some said that a tunnel ran from her place by the river all the way under the city; others said it just seemed that way because she moved so silently and quickly.

"But everyone knew about her songs. Her voice, sometimes sounding like a bird, sometimes like the whispering wind itself, soothed and comforted all who heard it. Listening to her song made anyone smile. She would sit by the water's edge at sunset and sing. Long after dark, her songs filled the night."

"What was her name?" asked Mimi.

"I think they called her Sun Spirit," whispered Mrs. Powell.

"That's a beautiful name," smiled Mimi.

"One night, the songs were silent," continued Mrs. Powell. "The folks who lived by the river searched for the old woman, but found only the ashes of an old camp fire and seven small, smooth stones."

At the mention of the seven stones, Rico and Ziggy stared at each other in amazement.

"So is she the ghost?" asked Jerome.

"No one knows, Jerome," Mrs. Powell replied quietly. "But late at night, after everyone has gone to bed, a strange whistling wind can be heard, blowing from the river and over the streets of Cincinnati. Sometimes it sounds like a voice; sometimes it sounds like a song."

The children shivered, even though the sun was warm and bright. "That was a good story," whispered Nicole.

Mrs. Powell stood up, looked at her watch, and announced, "It's about time to head for the boat, class. That's where we'll eat our lunch." Everyone stretched and walked slowly and quietly to the bus. Each child seemed to hold a little bit of the morning in his mind.

"Thanks, Mr. Greene," she added, "your knowledge about the past makes it all seem very real to us."

"It was my pleasure," smiled Mr. Greene. "And thank you, Mrs. Powell, for your story as well. The children will help us keep the old stories alive. We must never forget the past."

"Rashawn took my lunch!" screamed Tiana. "He said he was going to throw it in the river!"

"Rashawn, unless you plan to swim in the river to get her lunch back, give Tiana her lunch and get on the bus!" called Mrs. Powell.

"I was just playing," grinned Rashawn as he tossed Tiana her lunch bag. "I don't want her stinky old sandwich anyway!"

The short bus ride over the river and to the boat launch was forgotten as the class walked quickly down to the boat.

"Ooh yuk!" screamed Nicole. "I see a dead fish!"

"You'd be dead, too, if you had to swim in that polluted water where the boat docks, mon," said Ziggy.

JUICE
JUICE

The captain of the brightly painted *BB Riverboat* smiled as each student stepped off of the walkway and onto the boat. The boat was large enough to hold lots of people, but they had the boat to themselves this afternoon. There were tables set up for them to eat their lunches, and large open windows to view the river.

Jerome stood by the window, felt the soft river breeze, and smiled with satisfaction. "I should be a river boat captain! This is the life!"

Mr. Greene laughed. "Lots of people love the river and have made their living here. Go for it!"

Jerome, Rico, Rashawn, and Ziggy sat at a table together and ate lunch. The captain rattled off cheerful facts about the number of bridges and the depth of water while the boat chugged down the river. People from the shore waved as they passed by.

"Are we having a meeting of The Black Dinosaurs this week?" Rico asked dreamily as he stared at the water.

"I think we should," said Jerome. "We missed last week because of all that rain."

"Sure, mon," said Ziggy. "Saturday morning—ten o'clock."

"Sounds good to me," added Rashawn.

Rico liked to watch the sunlight dance on the ripples of the water. Jerome dreamed of fishing from the side of the boat. Ziggy hardly sat still, jumping up to see every new sight. Rashawn kept looking at Tiana, although he pretended to be looking for other boats on the river.

"I wonder if anybody tried to swim across the river to freedom," mused Mimi.

"Oh, yes, I'm sure some did," replied Mr. Greene. "And they had to swim at night, when it was dark and even more frightening."

"Wow, it sure is wide," observed Nicole.

"And terrifying!" added Mrs. Powell.

"Why do you think it's so scary, Mrs. P.?" asked Rico.

"Because I can't swim!" she admitted with an embarrassed grin.

Everyone laughed, and soon the boat returned to the dock. The tired children climbed back onto the bus with smiles of satisfaction. The ride back to school was quiet.

As Mr. Greene got off the bus to go home, several children called to him. "Thanks Mr. Greene. Come back again another day."

"I'll do that!" he grinned. "But first I have to rest up from this trip. Young people have too much energy for these old bones! Pay attention to your teachers, you hear? 'Bye now!"

"Good bye!"

Back in the classroom, Ziggy glanced at the clock. "Fifteen minutes before time to go home! Now that's my kind of school day, mon!"

Mrs. Powell had been in a good mood all day, but she still remembered to pass out the homework.

Jerome groaned. "What a terrible end to a wonderful day."

"If you give it a chance, I think you'll like this assignment," Mrs. Powell told Jerome and the rest of the class.

"What do we have to do?" asked Rashawn.

"You better give Ziggy two of those sheets, Mrs. Powell," teased Rico. "You know how he loses and forgets his homework!"

"You might be right, Rico," she laughed, as she handed Ziggy two of the assignment sheets.

"It's never my fault, mon," Ziggy laughed and tried to explain. But he took the two sheets anyway.

Mrs. Powell smiled at Ziggy and explained, "What I want you to do is write a story."

"A story? On what?" asked Nicole.

"I want you to call it 'FROM SLAVERY TO FREEDOM—A STORY OF ESCAPE.' I want you to make up a story about either a person who was trying to escape from slavery or a person who helped someone to escape," explained Mrs. Powell.

"You mean like Mr. Greene told us this morning?" asked Rico.

"Exactly!" replied Mrs. Powell. "But this time you are telling the story. Think about the river and think about the people in slavery. Then make up a story about escape."

"I think this is going to be fun," said Tiffany. "When do we have to turn it in?"

"Today is Thursday. Let's turn them in next Wednesday. If you like, you can read your story to the class."

"Don't forget now, Ziggy," Mrs. Powell gently reminded him. "No more excuses, OK?"

"When have I ever missed a homework?" Ziggy asked with fake innocence. The whole class groaned and laughed. At that, the bell rang, and the school day full of river memories came to an end.

Chapter 5

Saturday morning dawned cool and bright. Rico headed down the street towards Ziggy's house. "Hey, Rico!" yelled Jerome from across the street. "My grandma brought donuts for us!"

"Great! I'm starving. My mom quit buying donuts when she went on a diet. We have a house full of healthy food!"

They stopped in front of Rashawn's house. His dog, Afrika, slept on the front porch. He glanced at the boys, wagged his tail once, and went back to sleep. Rashawn hurried out of his front door, and tossed Afrika a dog biscuit as he jumped down the steps, two at a time. Afrika lifted his head, sniffed the biscuit, and seemed to ignore it, but he put his paw over it before he went back to sleep.

"Your dog is so lazy!" said Jerome.

"He's a retired police dog," explained Rashawn. "He spent his whole life chasing bad guys and finding missing people. He's like Mr. Greene—just sitting around and dreaming about the past. He's allowed to relax now."

Just then, Ziggy yelled to them from the end of the driveway which led to his backyard. "Hurry! Come back here! I have something to show you."

The three boys rushed across the street, and followed Ziggy around the corner of his house, down a path, and to their club house hidden in the back corner of his huge, tree-filled back yard. Breathless and laughing, the boys glanced over to see Afrika, asleep in the front of their clubhouse.

"How did he get here before we did?" asked Jerome.

"He knew where we were headed. He just took a short cut," explained Rashawn proudly. "I told you he was a police dog. He's really smart."

"Yeah, when he's not asleep!" teased Rico.

"So what's the big surprise, Ziggy?" asked Jerome.

"I found a clue to a secret from the past, mon!" replied Ziggy with excitement.

"What secret?"

"A clue? To what?"

Ziggy said with pretended seriousness, "We must first go inside and have an official meeting of The Black Dinosaurs. I say the password today is 'MYSTERIOUS!'"

Since Ziggy had a terrible memory and could never remember the official password, the other three always had fun making him remember it. "I bet he can't even remember his own password," smiled Rashawn.

Rico opened the door of the clubhouse. As he entered, each boy touched the huge, black plastic dinosaur that was hanging inside. Dusty leaves covered the floor and the breeze that blew through the holes in the wall that served as windows was slightly chilly.

"Looks like we need to sweep up a little," said Rashawn.

"Looks to me like we need to spray for bugs!" Jerome replied quickly. "It's been awhile since we've been here and spiders may not know they're not welcome!"

"We can do all that in a few minutes, mon" cried Ziggy. "Let me show you what I have!"

Rico couldn't wait any longer. "Show us!" he pleaded.

"First, tell me the password," Ziggy demanded.

"That's easy," said Jerome. "It's GHOST!"

Ziggy roared with pleasure. "Finally! Someone besides Ziggy forgot the password!"

"I know," Jerome grinned. "I was just messin' with you, Ziggy. Isn't the word MUSTARD?"

"It's MYSTERIOUS," laughed Rico. "Now what do you have to show us?"

Ziggy pulled a folded sheet of paper from his back pocket. He slowly unfolded it, smoothed it out, and placed it on the card table that Jerome's grandmother had given them. "It's a map!" he whispered with excitement.

"A treasure map?" asked Jerome hopefully.

"No, mon, a map of secrets!" replied Ziggy mysteriously. Ziggy now had their full attention. The map on the table was hand-drawn and it looked very old. It had lines and what looked like doorways, and the words "DESTROY THIS MAP!" written on the bottom.

"Where did you get it?" asked Rashawn.

Ziggy took a deep breath and began. "I got it from Mr. Greene. He got it from his grandfather. It should

have been destroyed long ago, because it could have meant death to anyone who was found with it.

"What is it a map of?" Rico wanted to know.

Ziggy paused dramatically. "It is a map of an Underground Railroad hiding place! Not only that—it's a map of the hiding places that are under our school!"

"Wow!" The rest of the guys were truly impressed. "Why would Mr. Greene give such a special map to you?"

"He didn't give it to me, mon. He just loaned it to me so I could get a good grade on my homework assignment. I was walking past his house yesterday while he was sitting on his porch, and we started talking, and he ended up digging this out of an old trunk. I have to give it back to him next week."

"So how is it going to help you do your homework?" asked Jerome.

"It's not gonna help at all, mon," replied Ziggy with a sly smile.

"Why not?"

"Because I can make up a story about an escaped slave out of my head, mon!"

"So what are you going to do with the map?"

asked Rashawn.

"It's not what *I'm* going to do with it; it's what *we're* going to do," said Ziggy, the excitement building in his voice.

"What's your plan, Ziggy?" asked Rico, who was beginning to see what Ziggy had in mind.

"We're going to follow this map and *find* the lost secret tunnel of the Underground Railroad that's hiding under our school!"

Chapter 6

"How do you think we're gonna find a lost tunnel? Those things have been hidden for over a hundred years!" sighed Rico.

"You know those old stairs behind the auditorium that lead to a brick wall, mon?" asked Ziggy.

"Sure," remembered Rashawn. "Last year when we were in the school play, we used to go down there and hide from the girls, and scare them when they came looking for us."

"There's a trapdoor back there also. It's built into the floor. But it has boxes over it and a big lock on it," added Jerome. "I used to wonder why the stairs went nowhere and why a trap door was hidden in the floor."

"The lock is open, mon!" announced Ziggy.

"What? How do you know?"

"Yesterday I was carrying some boxes for Mr. Lyon. He told me to put them in that storage area behind the stairs. And I noticed that *the lock was open*! It looked like it had just fallen apart because it was old."

"Did you tell anyone?"

"Of course not, mon! But I didn't think about that trapdoor and the hidden tunnels together until Mr. Greene gave me this map. I just know that there's a connection, mon!"

"What's the plan?" asked Rashawn.

"Mr. Lyon is having tryouts for this year's school play on Monday. Tell your parents that you're staying for that."

"I don't want to be in the play," complained Rico.

"You're only gonna be there so we can check out that trapdoor!" explained Jerome.

"Oh yeah! I get it! Good plan!"

"What should we bring?" asked Rashawn.

"Flashlights," suggested Rico, "with extra batteries!"

"Bug spray!" declared Jerome. "And some tools."

"Some rope and a couple of garbage bags," added Rashawn.

"And I'll bring the map and the 'Seven Special Stones of the Sun,' mon!" cried Ziggy.

"I don't think there's much sun where we're going," Rico remarked to Ziggy.

"Then that's all the more reason why we need them, mon! We'll meet in the school auditorium for play tryouts. Don't forget your supplies! The Black Dinosaurs are on the path of another adventure!"

School on Monday seemed to tiptoe in slow motion. A few students talked about the homework assignment. Tiffany Lawrence turned in her story early, typed and stapled. Ziggy, Rashawn, Rico, and Jerome had other things on their minds today. They met at lunch to make sure they had everything they needed.

"While the girls are trying out for their parts," Ziggy planned, "we'll see if we can get that trapdoor open. It shouldn't take long to just take a quick look and see what's down there, mon."

"Do you think it might be dangerous?" asked Rico, who tried to be thoughtful and practical.

"Not if we're very careful," explained Rashawn. "Besides, what could possibly happen in just a few minutes?"

Jerome agreed. The bell rang to get back to class, but The Black Dinosaurs waited for the bell to signal the end of the day.

When the students finally assembled in the auditorium for play tryouts, Mr. Lyon seemed pleased with the large turnout. "We'll have the tryouts for the female parts first," he announced. "Ladies, get your scripts and come to the stage, please."

The boys were restless and tired by the time Mr. Lyon got ready for the boys' tryouts. It was close to five o'clock, and almost dark outside. Rico tried out for the part of a young doctor who saved the lives of millions of people. Jerome tried out for the part of a young preacher who led his people to freedom. Rashawn tried out for the part of a great warrior who conquered many nations. And Ziggy tried out for the part of stage manager. "I like to be in charge, mon," he said with a grin.

Mr. Lyon thanked everyone for trying out, then dismissed everyone so he could lock up the building. He never even noticed that Ziggy, Rashawn, Rico, and Jerome, instead of leaving the building and heading for the late bus, moved quickly and quietly to the stairs behind the stage.

One of the girls, however, did notice. Tiana started to say something, but she didn't want to get them in trouble. She figured that Mr. Lyon would see them and chase them out of the building. Her mother arrived to pick her up then, and Tiana, after one last look at the big old school building, jumped in her mom's car and went home.

Rico and Rashawn easily moved the boxes off the top of the trap door. It was very old and looked as if it had not been opened for many years. The lock, as Ziggy had said, was broken. Jerome quietly removed the lock, and lifted the large iron handle on the trap-door.

"Give me a hand!" whispered Jerome.

Rashawn and Ziggy grabbed the handle also. "When I count to three—pull!" directed Rashawn.

"One—two—three—PULL!"

With a strange creaking noise, as if it were yawning, the old wooden trapdoor stretched and opened.

"Awesome, mon!" Ziggy exclaimed.

"Sh-sh-sh!" Rico reminded him. "We've got to be quiet!"

"What now?" asked Rashawn.

"There are steps leading down!" observed Rico

with fear in his voice.

"To where?" asked Jerome.

"Let's find out!" cried Ziggy. His face showed his usual cheerful grin, but his voice seemed a little shaky.

They got their flashlights out of their book bags and slowly peeped over the edge. The stairs leading down were made of wood. The air was very dusty and dry, but cool.

Ziggy went first. He put his foot on the first step. It creaked, but held his weight. Then he tried another step. And another. And another. Soon they could hardly see him.

"Come on down," cried Ziggy. "I think it's a hallway or a tunnel or something. I need more light. It's perfectly safe, mon—I think!"

Rashawn went down next, followed by Jerome, and finally Rico, who really didn't want to do this, but didn't want to disappoint his friends. At the bottom of the steps, they all turned on their flashlights and looked around.

They were in a small room. Boxes were stacked along the walls. Jerome looked closely at one of the boxes. "Look at the dates on these!" he said in amazement. The boxes read, "SCHOOL RECORDS—

1900–1909."

"This is no Underground Railroad tunnel," said Rashawn with disappointment. "It's just an old storage room for ancient school records. I bet no one in the school even knows that this room exists."

Rico still looked nervous. "Let's get out of here before we get in trouble!"

"You're right, mon," agreed Ziggy. "Hey, look at this—an old rope. I bet it was used by some old cowboys in a rodeo."

"Were there cowboys in Ohio?" asked Rico, who was starting to relax now that they were getting ready to leave.

"There were cows, weren't there? And boys? So I guess there could have been cowboys, mon! Watch me do a rope trick!"

Rashawn glanced over at Ziggy. Just as he started to yell, "ZIGGY—DON'T!!" Ziggy pulled the rope. The trapdoor slammed down with a loud and deafening THUD. Thick darkness surrounded them.

Chapter 7

Rico screamed. He was ready to cry. "I want to get out of here! Now!"

Jerome was breathing hard, but he said, "I'm the only one who didn't drop his flashlight. Let's find the others and turn them on. We just have to go back up the stairs and push the door open."

Jerome swept his light across the floor. Ziggy exclaimed, "Here's my flashlight, mon! But it won't come on. I think I broke it when I dropped it!"

Rashawn found his flashlight and turned it on. "Where's my book bag? I've got another flashlight in there." Rico turned on his own flashlight, found the spare, and gave it to Ziggy.

"Now what?" Rico asked. "I'm scared."

"Let's get that door open, and get out of here, mon! I'm with you." Even Ziggy had lost some of his usual good humor.

Jerome climbed the stairs and pushed. Nothing happened. "I need some help here," he called. Rico, then Rashawn, and finally Ziggy, all crowded on the narrow wooden steps, pushing with all their might. The door would not budge.

"Why won't it open?" asked Rico. He was starting to be really afraid. He didn't like closed-in places and he didn't want the other boys to know that he was afraid of the dark.

"Do you think anyone could hear us if we yell?" asked Jerome.

"Probably not. We're behind the storage area of the stage. Nobody is even going to come back here. Everybody is on their way home!"

"So let's try to get someone's attention before everybody leaves!" said Rashawn. "Maybe Mr. Lyon will come back here to check the lights or something."

They knocked and yelled and screamed. Nothing happened. Rico couldn't help it. He started to cry. "It's OK, mon," Ziggy said gently. "We'll get out of here. Don't worry." But Ziggy sounded worried.

Rashawn finally said, "There's got to be another way out of here. Let's go down that hall. They took their flashlights and book bags, and slowly walked into the darkness. The walls were thick with dust and spider webs.

Rico, still sniffling, followed closely behind Rashawn.

Jerome said fearfully, "These webs are getting all in my hair. I think I'm gonna scream! If you see a spider, just don't tell me, OK?"

Ziggy, trying very hard to find his lost sense of adventure, was too scared to crack a joke. At the end of the short hallway was a door. "Let's try it, mon. What have we got to lose?"

The door was unlocked. It opened to a small room, empty except for a broken chair. Near the floor on the far wall, a hole had been dug. It was about three feet high. "I think we should see where it leads," suggested Rashawn.

Rashawn crawled through first. The hole led to a tunnel made of hard packed earth. "Should we try it? It looks really long. I can't see the end of it."

"Suppose there's monsters or rats or dead things?" asked Rico fearfully. "Or ghosts?"

"We'll just have the monsters and ghosts to gobble up the rats and dead things, OK mon?" Ziggy said, trying to cheer Rico.

"So how will that get rid of the monsters and ghosts?"

"I don't know, mon, but at least they won't be hungry!"

Rico smiled a little, and said, "Let's go for it."

In single file, on their hands and knees, The Black Dinosaurs crawled through the dirt tunnel, their flashlights the only gleam in the darkness. They were frightened, dirty, and hungry. They crawled slowly because they were very afraid and the tunnel was quite long. They moved cautiously, bumping each other and feeling the tightness of the tunnel on their bodies.

"Isn't this ever gonna end?" moaned Rico. "I know we've been in here an hour or more!"

Finally Rashawn, who was in the lead, exclaimed, "We're coming to the end of the tunnel!"

"At last!" yelled Rico with cheer.

One by one they crawled into a large, earthen room. "Where are we?" asked Jerome.

"You know what, mon?" said Ziggy. "I think we really have found one of those secret hiding places from the Underground Railroad!"

The walls of the room were made of hard-packed

dirt. It was tall enough for the boys to stand up in and big enough for the four of them to move around comfortably. It was very silent and smelled of old wood and rich earth.

"I think you're right, Ziggy. Look at this!" cried Rashawn. He had found a small bundle of what at first looked like rags.

"What is it?" asked Rico, shining his flashlight in that direction.

Rashawn looked closely at the bundle. "It's not rags—it's a shirt of some kind. And look—I think this is a cooking pot!"

"This might have been a weapon," Ziggy said dramatically, holding up a rounded wooden stick.

"It looks like a slingshot—it was probably used to kill more rabbits than enemies," added Jerome.

"But an escaped slave would have had lots of very bad enemies, right mon?" Ziggy insisted.

"Sure, Ziggy," agreed Jerome.

"Do you think this stuff belonged to a real escaped slave?" asked Rico.

"I think so," replied Jerome, as he touched the bundle gently. "Look! What's this?" Tied in a smaller bundle were seven smooth stones.

"Awesome, mon," whispered Ziggy. "We've found a real live tunnel of the Underground Railroad! I bet these stones belonged to a kid like us."

"Do you think this stuff could have belonged to Mr. Greene's grandfather?" asked Rashawn.

"It's possible," Rico replied. "I don't feel so scared knowing that this stuff belonged to someone who's like a friend to us."

"Won't this be a wonderful gift to give to Mr. Greene when we get out of here, mon?" suggested Ziggy.

"You mean *if* we get out of here," groaned Rico.

"Think positive, mon!" Ziggy was trying to remain cheerful. He then took his own seven stones from his book bag and placed them gently and carefully around the bundle. "These are for you, mon," he said quietly, "whoever you are."

"Just think," added Jerome, "escaped slaves slept here and hid here and worried if someone would find them."

Ziggy exclaimed suddenly, "Turn off all your flashlights!"

"Why? Are you crazy?"

"Just for a minute, mon! I want to see something."

"What do you think you're going to see in the dark?"

"Just do it. One—two—three—OFF!"

The darkness was sudden and total. It seemed to grab the boys and squeeze the breath from them. Rico screamed again.

"This is what it was like!" whispered Ziggy. "When the escaped slaves were hiding here, this is the darkness that covered them, mon!"

"Wow!" whispered Rico. "They were braver than I'll ever be! Let's turn the lights back on!"

The beams of the four flashlights seemed like bright sunshine after that breath-grabbing darkness. Each boy breathed a little easier.

"Where's that map, Ziggy?" asked Rashawn.

Ziggy dug down in his book bag and pulled out the old map. With the four flashlights shining on it, the map looked mysterious and seemed to glow in the darkness.

"I think we're right here," said Jerome, pointing to a small square on the map. "See, here's the tunnel we just crawled through."

"Is there a way out?" asked Rico. "I want to go home!"

"According to this," said Rashawn, "there's one more tunnel—and if I'm looking at this right, it leads right down to the river!"

Chapter 8

"The river?" asked Rico fearfully.

"If Mr. Greene was right," Jerome said thoughtfully, "the escaped slaves would have to hide again as soon as they crossed the river. It makes sense that a tunnel would run from the river to a safe house."

"Didn't Mrs. Powell talk about a tunnel in that ghost story?" asked Jerome.

"Don't start talking about ghosts," warned Rico. "I'm scared enough already!"

The light from Ziggy's flashlight suddenly flickered and fluttered out. Rico gasped with fear. The darkness seemed to get larger with only three small beams of light remaining. "Who brought extra batteries, mon?" Ziggy asked hopefully.

"I meant to, but I forgot."

"Me, too."

"So did I."

"Well, we're down to three lights. Let's find that last tunnel and get out of here, mon!"

Rico, who felt the darkness more than the others, scrambled to his knees and started checking the wall near the floor for loose spots. "I found something!" he yelled suddenly.

Another earthen tunnel led from the room and waited for the boys to discover its mysteries. Ziggy took a deep breath and crawled in first this time. The others followed closely behind. No one spoke much. Even Ziggy was quiet.

The earth in this tunnel was loose and damp. It crumbled as they crawled. "Can you see anything ahead?" Rico asked Ziggy.

"No, just more darkness, mon."

Suddenly Ziggy screamed. Jerome, who was right behind him, bumped into Ziggy and yelled, "What was that?"

"I think it was a rat, mon! It ran right past us!"

Rico whispered over and over, "I want to go home. I want to go home. I want to go home."

They continued slowly through the tunnel, the dirt becoming mud that squished through their fingers.

"I think I see a light ahead!" yelled Ziggy.

"Do you think it's a way out of here?" asked Rashawn.

"I'm scared," admitted Jerome. "Suppose there's no way out and we're stuck here forever!"

"Stop talking like that!" yelled Rico. "Ziggy, what do you see?"

"It couldn't be a street light, mon," Ziggy reasoned. "It must be some kind of light that is used when the sewers are checked."

"If we're near the sewers by the river, we're close to a way out!" exclaimed Jerome.

"All right! YES!" they all cheered loudly. Ziggy was so glad and so excited that he forgot that they were in a narrow tunnel and he tried to stand up. His head bumped the top of the tunnel and his outstretched hand knocked the side of the tunnel wall. Suddenly, with a thunderous roar, the wet dirt that had been holding the tunnel together for over a hundred years collapsed. Dirt and darkness covered the four trembling boys.

Rico, terrified of the darkness, cried, "Help! I can't see!"

Rashawn and Jerome coughed and screamed, reaching out, trying to find each other in the thick blackness.

Ziggy shook the dirt from his head and face and

felt a flashlight under his foot. He reached for it and quickly turned it on. The thin beam of light flickered weakly. The four boys sat huddled together in a space just large enough for the four of them.

Mud and tears streaked their frightened faces. The tunnel that they had just come through was completely collapsed. It was now just a huge pile of muddy dirt. The end of the tunnel that seemed to lead to that light they had seen earlier was also blocked with dirt and debris.

"There's no way out, mon," whispered Ziggy with fear. "We're trapped!"

"Is that another one of our flashlights?" asked Rico hopefully. A faint whisper of light filtered through the rocks and mud.

"No!" cried Rashawn. That's the light we saw earlier! Let's see if we can move some of this stuff. Who brought the tools?"

"I did," replied Jerome.

"Good, get them out!"

"I can't."

"Why not?" asked Rico with rising fear.

"Because my book bag is under all that dirt and mud. I don't even know where to look."

They all sighed. "Let's just use our hands, mon," suggested Ziggy. "Maybe we can dig an opening big enough for one of us to get through."

They took turns digging with their hands, but were only able to make a small opening. They could see a faint light in the distance, but the hole was only big enough for a hand, not a boy, to fit through.

"Do you think anyone is looking for us?" asked Rico. "My mom is gonna be really worried when I don't get off the late bus. I always call her if I'm gonna be late."

"What time is it anyway?"

"I don't know. Nobody has a watch."

"It's getting really late—it seems like we've been in here a *really* long time."

"I'm hungry!" moaned Rico.

"Me too," agreed Rashawn. "Ziggy, what do you have in your book bag?"

"I'm not sure, mon. Not much. All I have are some broken pencils, a green tennis shoe, and . . . wait!—I forgot I had this—it's my sandwich from lunch!"

They all cheered as Ziggy carefully unwrapped his sandwich.

"What's that green, lumpy stuff?" asked Jerome,

who wrinkled his nose.

"Oh, that's the broccoli," said Ziggy cheerfully.

"Broccoli?" jeered Rashawn. "On a sandwich?"

"Sure," grinned Ziggy. "Doesn't everybody eat broccoli and potato chip sandwiches?"

They groaned and laughed in spite of themselves. Ziggy broke the sandwich into four pieces. It was surprisingly delicious.

"That's the best sandwich I ever had in my life!" exclaimed Rico as he licked his fingers.

"We gotta get out of here," laughed Jerome. "When Ziggy's food starts to taste good, we're in serious trouble."

Ziggy's mood brightened a bit as he had an idea. "Let's toss the rest of this stuff through the hole. Maybe someone will see them and find us."

"Yeah, in a million years!" said Rashawn with a sigh.

"It can't hurt," Rico said weakly. He was willing to do anything at this point.

Each boy took an item from Ziggy's book bag and silently tossed it through the hole—two paper clips, the broken flashlight, several broken pencils, last week's lunch menu—taking turns until everything

was gone. The only thing left in Ziggy's book bag was his green tennis shoe. With a shrug, he tossed that, too.

"Why not, mon?"

"Where's the match to that shoe, Ziggy?" asked Rashawn.

"I think it's at your house, mon. I left it there that day we took our shoes off to play in the rain."

Suddenly, the last flashlight finally flickered out and the damp, wet darkness, like a shadowy monster, gobbled them up.

Chapter 9

Rico started to scream again, but the darkness seemed to silence all sound. Their hearts beat wildly and all four boys were close to tears.

"I can't stand this darkness!" cried Rico. "I want to go home! I want my mother!"

"My granny's warm blankets sure would feel good right now," mused Jerome.

"I wonder if I'll ever see my mum again," mumbled Ziggy.

"I'm really scared," Rashawn admitted. "What if we never get out?"

No one had an answer. There was nothing more to say. The boys sat silently in the darkness, listening to the darkness and thinking of brighter days. Time seemed to tiptoe.

Only their rapid breathing and faint sniffling

could be heard at first. Then softly, slowly, faintly they heard the sound of a pale whistling wind, almost like a song. They could feel no breeze, but they knew that the wind surrounded them and it soothed them.

"What is it?" whispered Rico.

"It's just the wind," Rashawn said softly.

"No, it's like—a song or something," added Jerome.

"I think it's the ghost, mon!" Ziggy breathed quietly. "It's Sun Spirit! She's tellin' us not to worry. We're gonna be OK."

"The ghost?" whispered Rico.

"I just have a feeling, mon," repeated Ziggy. "Can't you feel it, too? It's the River City Ghost!"

Jerome looked at Rashawn; they felt it, too. But they were not afraid. The four boys shivered, then grinned.

"Awesome, mon!" breathed Ziggy.

No one argued with Ziggy. The strange breeze seemed to calm their fears and helped them relax. It was like a song that warmed them from the inside out. The four friends sat huddled together in the darkness, frightened, lost, but somehow not completely alone. They slept. They dreamed.

Rico dreamt of a large, white house with tall, graceful columns in the front. It was surrounded by graceful trees and was filled with lovely old furniture and decorations. From behind the house, sad songs could be heard. On the wide, white marble steps in the front of the house sat a small brown boy, crying. His mother walked toward him, wiped his tears and hugged him. She whispered softly, "Tonight . . . tonight. . . ."

Rashawn dreamt of dogs—just like his dog—but huge and mean and chasing him. He was running through the woods and he didn't have on any shoes. Rocks kept sticking his feet and branches scratched his legs. His side hurt from running and his heart was beating fast. The sun was going down and he knew he could hide in the darkness. But he felt strong because his dad was holding his hand, running with him. He knew he would not fall. "Tonight," he thought. "Tonight."

Jerome dreamt of two little girls who looked just like his sisters. They were in the Ohio River and were trying to swim. A huge boat with a loud horn was moving swiftly through the dark water, getting nearer and nearer to the wet and frightened girls. He tried to reach them, but the water was deep and cold. His granny appeared from beneath the waves and floated nearby, smiling. She wasn't even wet. He heard his granny say, "We'll rescue them tonight . . . tonight."

Ziggy dreamt of birds. He was a huge golden eagle, flying in the sunlight, in the bright, clear air. He could see for miles and his strong wings soared with freedom and pride. He did rolls and dives and laughed out loud as he flew upside-down just for fun. The earth and the air belonged to him and he shouted to the sun, "Today! Today!"

Gradually the cold and the cramped conditions awakened the four sleeping boys. Jerome wiggled his arm because he thought he felt a spider crawling on it. Rashawn's long legs felt like pretzels and Rico really needed to go to the bathroom.

Suddenly Ziggy screamed. "What was that?" he gasped.

Fear grabbed the boys once again as they listened to a terrifying rumble in the distance. It was a grinding, growling noise that seemed ready to destroy them.

"What could that be?" screamed Jerome.

"It's the ghost!" yelled Rashawn. "It's gonna get us!"

"The ghost is not mean, mon. It's gotta be something else! Maybe it's a monster," added Ziggy with fear. "Monsters live underground, you know."

"What are we going to do?" screamed Rico.

They couldn't move in the small cave-like area that they were trapped in. They huddled together in the darkness, listening in fear.

From the other side of the small opening they had made the terrifying sound grew louder and closer and more dangerous. It was the growling and scraping of a very large animal.

"It sounds like a bear!" cried Rico.

"There are no bears in the sewer, Rico. No, I think it's a huge rat!" Jerome said quietly.

"It's getting closer!" cried Rashawn with terror.

Each boy spoke softly, for their fear of the darkness and fear of the approaching animal made them afraid to move, afraid to even breathe.

The scraping and sniffing and growling sounds were right outside the opening now. Whatever it was had wet fur, for the terrified boys could smell its damp animal odor.

It scraped and dug furiously near the opening. The hole got larger. Large hunks of dirt fell away in a loud thudding crash, and the huge, wet, black animal bounded into the small area where the four boys huddled together.

They screamed.

It headed first for Rashawn. He could feel its hot breath approaching. Then it licked his face.

"It's Afrika!" Rashawn screamed with relief and happiness. "Where'd you come from, boy? How did you find us?"

"I knew we'd be rescued, mon!" exclaimed Ziggy with joy. "I was never even worried!"

Rico was more honest. "I've never been so glad to see that big, old, stinky dog in my life! I'll never call him lazy again! I promise."

The dog ran from boy to boy, licking their dirty faces, and letting them hug him. He seemed to know that they were lost and that they needed to feel safe again.

Ziggy exclaimed with a bit of his usual cheerful attitude, "Rashawn, let's follow this wonderful dog of yours out of here, mon!"

Everyone agreed and the four boys quickly scrambled through the hole and down a steep hill. Afrika barked once or twice as he led them to what they could see was a sewer tunnel. He ran back and forth, making sure that each boy was following.

When they reached the sewer, they could hear voices coming from above. Rashawn's dad was saying, "I hear the dog barking!"

Rashawn cried out, "Dad! Dad! We're down here!"

His dad, with relief in his voice, answered loudly, "Rashawn! Are you OK? Are the other boys with you?"

"Yes, Dad. We're all here, and we're fine now. Afrika found us and saved us!"

Rico's mom then shouted through the small sewer opening. He could tell she had been crying. "Rico! Are you there? Are you OK, baby?"

Rico wasn't even embarrassed to let the other boys know his mom called him baby. He had never heard anything more wonderful in his life. "I'm fine, Momma. We're all OK, really!"

"Stand back, boys," boomed the loud voice of Rashawn's father. "Here comes the jack hammer. They're going to open the sewer entrance so you can get out. This will be loud, but it will only take a few minutes."

The sound of the jackhammer breaking the steel and concrete of the sewer pipe was loud and pounding and rattled the boys to their bones. The silence when it stopped was sudden.

"Ziggy? You down there boy?" Ziggy's mom shouted with worry in her voice.

"Oh, my mum!" Ziggy cried with a whoop of delight. He was the first to crawl out of the sewer and up to the street.

Jerome followed, with Rico and Rashawn right behind him. Jerome ran to his grandmother, hugged her with all his might, and finally broke down and cried. He even hugged his two little sisters.

The boys looked around in amazement at the crowd of people who stood cheering and clapping as they climbed out of the sewer. Rico's mother, Rashawn's parents, Jerome's grandmother, and Ziggy's parents and uncles all hugged the boys, the worry on their faces replaced by joy.

In addition, rescue crews with large digging equipment, two fire trucks, several police cars, an ambulance, and a television news truck were

assembled. Mr. Greene, Mr. Lyon, and Mrs. Powell stood together. Several students from their class at school were also there with their parents. Tiana smiled shyly at Rashawn. This time he smiled back.

Chapter 10

Wrapped in blankets and sipping hot chocolate, the four friends sat in the back of an ambulance, a little overwhelmed by all the attention. Mr. Greene and Mrs. Powell walked over to the boys On their faces was that look that grownups use when a kid is in trouble—a little angry, but smiling at the same time.

"What got into you fellas? Ziggy, if I thought you boys were going to try to follow that map, I never would have loaned it to you," scolded Mr. Greene.

"We were just going to look around a little, mon," explained Ziggy, speaking very fast. "Then the door got stuck and we couldn't get out, and we got scared, and we followed the map until the tunnel caved in!"

"How did you find us?" asked Rashawn.

"At first, when your parents started calling the school and your friends because the four of you were not home yet, we had no idea where you might be," explained Mrs. Powell.

"Then Tiana told your parents that she saw the four of you go back stage, but she didn't remember seeing you come out. She thought that maybe you might be up to something."

"When Mrs. Powell called me to let me know that you boys were missing, I knew it had something to do with that map," added Mr. Greene.

"We unjammed the trapdoor and followed your path until we got to the cave-in," Mr. Lyon said with fear still in his voice. "That's when everyone got really worried and we called the police and rescue crews."

"We heard the ghost, Mrs. Powell," Rico said quietly. "She's real, and she lives down there. I think she must have been a real comfort to the escaped slaves hiding in the darkness."

"Ghost?" Mrs. Powell replied with wonder. "That's just an old story from long ago. You probably just heard the wind."

The four boys looked at each other and smiled. They knew that the whistling song they had heard was more than just wind. They had been touched by a voice from the past.

"Did you find the bundle in the Underground Railroad tunnel?" asked Jerome with excitement.

"We sure did," replied Mrs. Powell. "You have stumbled across a secret that's been hidden for almost a hundred and fifty years! It's a very important, very valuable historical find."

"Wait till you read my report, Mrs. Powell," grinned Ziggy with a twinkle in his eye. "Now we *really* know what it's like to travel on the Underground Railroad."

"It's dark, and it's scary, and it's dangerous!" exclaimed Rashawn. "Whoever left that small bundle was a very brave person."

"Mr. Greene, do you think it might have belonged to your Grandpa Mac?" asked Jerome.

"I don't know, Jerome," replied Mr. Greene, "but I sure would like to think so."

"What's gonna happen to that stuff we found, mon?" Ziggy asked as he stirred his hot chocolate with a pickle.

"Let's call the African-American Museum in Wilberforce, Ohio," suggested Mrs. Powell. "I'm sure that it will receive a place of honor in a display there."

"That's cool, mon."

Rico said quietly, "I didn't think we would ever get out of there. How did you know where to find us on the other side?"

Rashawn's dad hugged his son once again and replied, "We knew that the tunnel probably ran down to the sewer lines and then down to the river. But we weren't sure where to look. Mr. Greene gave us a general idea, but it was Afrika who found you."

"He squeezed through a small opening in the sewer line and came back with one green tennis shoe," added Mr. Greene.

"My green shoe, mon!" shouted Ziggy with glee. "That was part of my secret rescue plan!"

"Afrika then went back and dug until he found you," explained Rashawn's dad. "He's a real hero."

"Where is Afrika?" asked Jerome. "We haven't seen him since he found us."

"Look, mon," said Ziggy with a laugh.

Curled up in the front seat of the ambulance, with a green tennis shoe under his paw, Afrika, ignoring all the noise and confusion, was fast asleep.

Chapter 11
Ziggy's Report

Seven Smooth Stones

by Ziggy Colwin

Traveling on the Underground Railroad was a really scary thing. A boy named Mac ran away from slavery with his mother. They wanted to be free, so they walked three hundred miles to Ohio. It took a long time because they could only move at night. It was very dark and they heard sounds that made Mac want to cry, but he didn't. In the daytime slave catchers were looking for them, so they had to hide in the bushes or in barns of people who helped them. It was summer time so it was hot and when bugs bit him, he couldn't even scratch. Even a sneeze was dangerous. When Mac and his mum got to Cincinnati, they hid in a tunnel under a house. Mac didn't get to play very much. All he had was a slingshot and seven smooth stones. But Mac was a brave boy who didn't know that he was going to be famous. But I know. I was there.

The End

Glossary

ancient *(adjective)* very old (p. 53)

architect *(noun)* someone who designs buildings and makes sure they're built the right way (p. 7)

cease *(verb)* to stop (p. 4)

daring *(adjective)* risky (p. 19)

deafening *(adjective)* very loud (p. 53)

debris *(noun)* pieces of something that has broken apart (p. 66)

dramatically *(adverb)* with great feeling (p. 25)

method *(noun)* a way of doing something (p. 19)

mysterious *(adjective)* very hard to explain or understand (p. 19)

practical *(adjective)* showing good judgement (p. 47)

route *(noun)* a path or course (p. 14)

severely *(adverb)* harshly (p. 22)

soothe *(verb)* to calm someone down (p. 29)

terrifying *(adjective)* very scary (p. 34)